Ben and the Outer-Space Race

Justin Scott Parr

GumshoePress

All rights reserved, including the reproduction of this book or portions thereof in any form whatsoever except as provided by the U.S. Copyright Law.

This is a work of fiction. Names, characters, places, and incidents are either the product of the author's imagination or, if real, are used fictitiously.

Text copyright © 2016 Justin Scott Parr
Illustrations and artwork copyright © 2016 GumshoePress

Editor: Carrie White
Illustrated by: Igor Adasikov
Cover Art by: Igor Adasikov, Afreena Rahman
Cover Design by: Svetlana Uscumlic
Interior Design by: Evie Baldwin

ISBN: 978-1-939001-54-2

Please purchase only authorized editions and do not participate in or encourage piracy of copyrighted materials. Your support of the author's rights is appreciated.

Books may be purchased in bulk at special discounts for promotional or educational purposes. Inquiries for sales, distribution, and permissions should be addressed to:

GumshoePress
P.O. Box 1332
New York, NY 10163
support@gumshoepress.com
www.gumshoepress.com

He blasted off inside a spaceship.

"Hi, Ben!" the star said. "Would you like to race around the Solar System?"

"Okay," Ben answered. "But how can we race in outer space?"

"With bikes, boats, and planes," the star said. "Just use your imagination. Ready. Set. *Go!*"

Ben watched the star shoot ahead, but he didn't see where it went.

So he took an elevator to the Sun.

"Hi, Sun, did you see a shooting star?"

"It went in that direction," the Sun said.

Next, Ben floated inside a balloon above Mercury.

"Wow, I got here fast," said Ben.

"That's because I'm the closest planet to the sun," Mercury said.

He flew an airplane to Venus.

"This planet looks like home," Ben said.

"Because Earth is my twin," Venus replied.

He peddled a bicycle past Earth.

"I'll be back after I catch the star!" Ben shouted.

"Good luck!" said Earth.

"And safe travels!" the moon added.

He steered a rover to Mars.

"You just missed the shooting star," said the red planet. "Look, it's over there!"

He paddled a boat to the next planet.

"Where am I now?" Ben wondered.

"You can always recognize me," said Jupiter, "because I have a great red spot."

He hopped across the Asteroid Belt.

"Has anyone seen a shooting star?" he asked.

"It went that way!" said the asteroids.

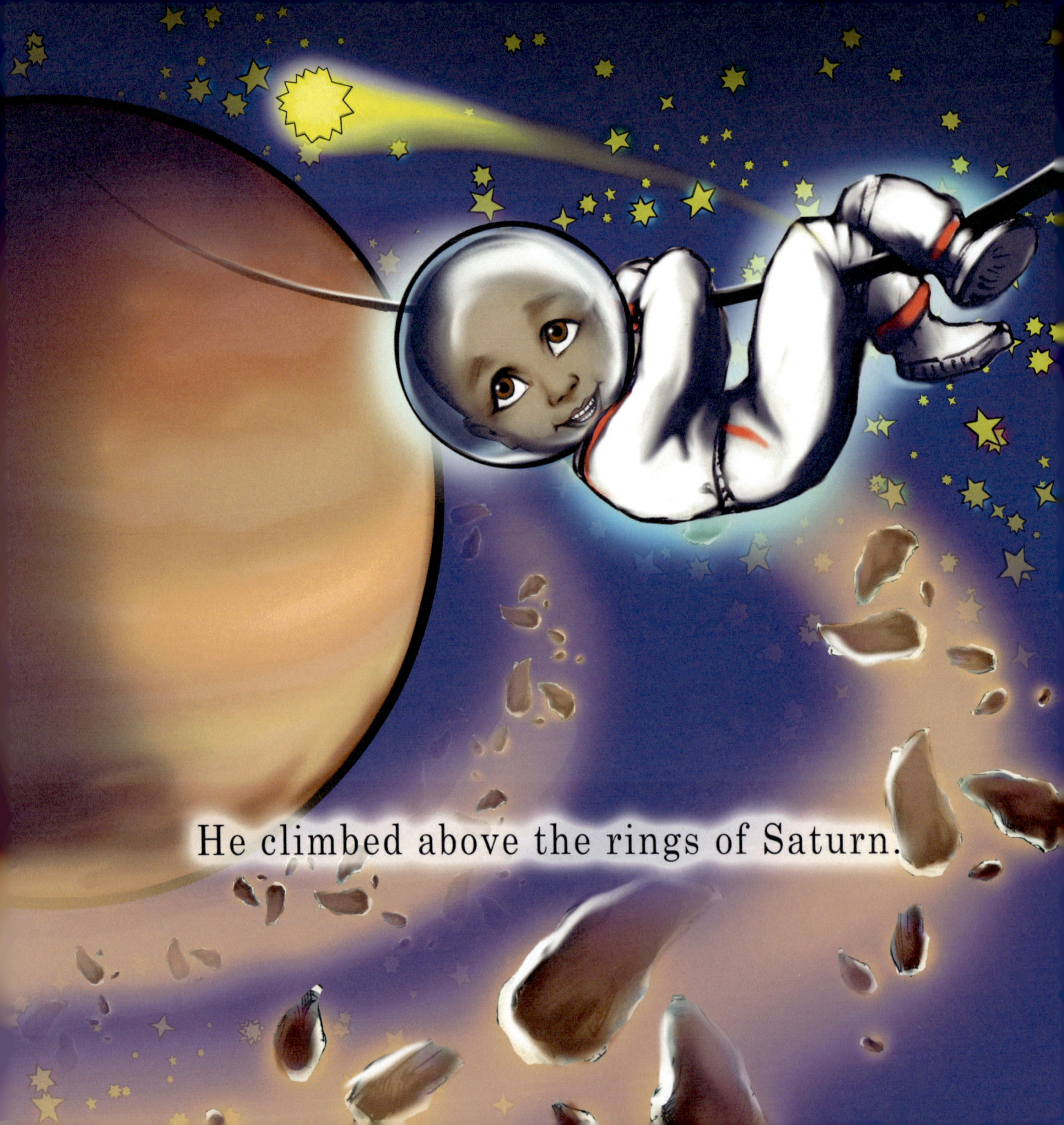

He skied the frozen mountains of Neptune.

"Wow, that star is fast," said Ben. "But *I'm* faster!"

Ben rode a scooter toward Pluto.

"Oh no," he said. "This is the last planet in the Solar System!"

"Well, some people say I'm just a dwarf," Pluto replied. "Hurry, Ben, this is your final chance to catch the star!"

Ben stood on his tiptoes, reached out, and . . .

"You saved me!" the star said. "Tonight, I will shine extra bright just for you."

Ben placed the star back into the sky. "Be more careful next time," he said.

And that night . . .

To Parents and Educators

The following resources are intended to supplement your child's understanding of the concepts in Ben and the Outer-Space Race. Enjoy these fact pages, craft ideas, outdoor activities, and snack options related to astronomy.

DID YOU KNOW...

- Astronomy is the study of stars, planets, asteroids, comets, and other objects in outer space. Astronomers are the scientists who study astronomy.
- Our Solar System includes the Sun and all the objects that orbit around it, including eight planets: Mercury, Earth, Venus, Mars, Jupiter, Saturn, and Uranus. Pluto was once considered a planet, but now it is not.
- Only one moon orbits Earth, but there are more than 170 other moons throughout our Solar System.
- The Sun is actually a star—the only star in our Solar System—and it's over 300,000 times bigger than Earth.
- Earth is 93 million miles away from the Sun, and it takes about 8 minutes for light to travel from the Sun to Earth.
- Mercury is the closest planet to the Sun, yet Venus is the hottest planet in our Solar System with a surface temperature of over 840°F.
- Uranus is the coldest planet in the solar system. Astronomers often refer to it as the "Ice Giant."
- Mars is home to Olympus Mons, the tallest volcano in the Solar System. Mars is also known as the "Red Planet" due to the color of the iron in its soil.
- The asteroid belt is located between Mars and Jupiter. The belt is made of thousands of objects; some are no larger than a grain of dust, while others are more than 100 miles across and even have their own moons!
- Jupiter is the largest planet in the Solar System. It is so big that Earth could fit inside of it 1,000 times. Jupiter is known for its "Great Red Spot" which is actually a massive storm that has lasted over 300 years!
- Saturn is easy to identify because of its rings, which are made of ice particles, rocks, and dust.
- Neptune is so far from the Sun that it takes 165 years for the planet to orbit the Sun one time.

THE TRUTH ABOUT "SHOOTING STARS"

Shooting stars aren't really stars at all. In fact, they're tiny bits of dust, dirt, and rocks—called meteors—which travel through space to Earth. These particles move at speeds faster than race cars and crash into Earth's atmosphere. But don't worry; they won't hurt you. Each tiny particle burns up when it enters Earth's atmosphere, which is why you see a bright flash of light streak across the sky.

Observe the Solar System

HERE IS WHAT YOU NEED:
A copy of the SKY CHART for each person

- Do this activity with your parents.
- Fill in the date.
- Write 'starry' or 'cloudy' to describe each night.
- Put an X in the boxes marked big and little dipper if you can find them.
- Write down the names of the other constellations and planets you can find.

HERE IS WHAT YOU DO:
- Have your child fill out the chart each evening for a week.
- Discuss and chart the results using the completed SKY CHART summary below:

SKY CHART QUESTIONS
1. Which night of the week had the most stars?
2. Which night of the week had the fewest stars?
3. How many nights were there few or no stars?
4. How many constellations were you able to identify each night?
5. Which ones did you find?
6. Which star is part of the handle of the little dipper?
7. Did you see any planets?
8. Did you see any "shooting stars"?

SKY CHART

DATE	STARRY OR CLOUDY	BIG DIPPER	LITTLE DIPPER	OTHER CONSTELLATIONS	PLANETS

Let's Eat!

MAKE THE FOLLOWING TREATS WITH YOUR CHILD:

CLOUDY WITH A CHANCE OF STARS
Fill 4- to 8-oz. clear plastic cups with either whipped topping or vanilla yogurt mixed with star-shaped sprinkles or marshmallow bits. Serve with a spoon and enjoy!

SPACE BISCUITS
Roll out a can of biscuits to make one large crust, using one crust for every 6 people. Bake at 350°F until done. Immediately spread a thin layer of chocolate icing on the crust and add sliced kiwi, bananas, strawberries, grapes, and marshmallows. Serve for dessert, and talk about the planets and stars.

TO THE MOON AND BEYOND
Cut strips from canned crescent rolls or homemade dough and wrap them around hot dogs, leaving parts of the hot dog showing through. Make a slit in one end of the hot dog, insert a triangular-shaped snack cracker, and bake until the dough is browned. Serve with cheese ball 'stars' or cheese cubes.

FRUITY ROCKET SHIPS
Arrange banana chunks onto bamboo skewers, and top with watermelon chunks cut in the shape of a triangle to form the tip of the rocket.

All translations and audiobooks are produced by NATIVE EDITORS and PROFESSIONAL NARRATORS.

EDUCATORS around the world praise Ben as an effective resource for teaching foreign languages to kids.

LANGUAGES:
- English
- Spanish
- Portuguese
- German
- French
- Italian
- Japanese

Made in the USA
Monee, IL
28 April 2026

49137076R00029